Samuel C. Clarke

Records of Some of the Descendants of John Fuller, Newton, 1644-98

SALZWASSER
VERLAG

Samuel C. Clarke

Records of Some of the Descendants of John Fuller, Newton, 1644-98

Reprint of the original, first published in 1869.

1st Edition 2022 | ISBN: 978-3-37502-152-8

Verlag (Publisher): Salzwasser Verlag GmbH, Zeilweg 44, 60439 Frankfurt, Deutschland
Vertretungsberechtigt (Authorized to represent): E. Roepke, Zeilweg 44, 60439 Frankfurt, Deutschland
Druck (Print): Books on Demand GmbH, In de Tarpen 42, 22848 Norderstedt, Deutschland

RECORDS

OF SOME OF THE

DESCENDANTS OF JOHN FULLER,

NEWTON, 1644-98.

Compiled from Jackson's History of Newton, and other sources.

BY

SAMUEL C. CLARKE.

———

BOSTON:
PRINTED BY DAVID CLAPP & SON.
1869.

FULLERS OF NEW ENGLAND.

In the Mayflower came Edward Fuller, and Dr. Samuel Fuller. Edward died in the great mortality, 1621, leaving only son Samuel, who settled on the Cape. Dr. Samuel Fuller died in 1633, leaving an only son Samuel, who became minister of Middleboro', and died there in 1695, aged 71.

1. JOHN FULLER, supposed to have come with J. Winthrop, Jr., in the Abigail, Hackwell, master, in 1635, was born in England in 1620.* He settled in Cambridge village (now Newton), in 1644. In Dec., 1658, he purchased of Joseph Cooke, of Cambridge, 750 acres of land in the Northwest part of Newton, for 160 pounds sterling. It was bounded North and West by Charles river, East by land of Thomas Park, and South by S. Shepard's farm. His house stood on the South side of the road, and West side of the brook, within a few rods of both. By subsequent purchases he increased his tract to upwards of 1000 acres. Edward Jackson and John Fuller were the largest land-holders in the town. Cheese-cake brook ran through this tract, which was long known as the "Fuller Farm." He divided it among his five sons by will (son Isaac having died in 1691), with the proviso that they should not sell to any stranger, until they or their next relative should have the offer of it. Twenty-two of John Fuller's descendants were in the army of the Revolution, from Newton.†

The following document, apparently in John Fuller's handwriting, is in the possession of a descendant:

"Wee whose names are subscribed are able to give this theire testimony that when the land was sould to Ensign John Spring

---

* In the Abigail, Hackwell master, May 4 1635, came Wm. Fuller 25; Jo. Fuller 15.
—James Savage's Note in "Historical Collections."
† Jackson's *History of Newton.*

liveing in New Towne in the County of Middelsexe in New England that there was Reserved a high waye, Through his land for
the use of the Inhabitanc of the saide town to pass in namely the
highway for————in the place where it was then occupied
and if the said John Spring did fence in the said land he should
hang gates. And this is so to be understood of ye. land which
ye above said John Spring now lives upon.

New Towne december
John Fuller *Senect.*   15 1691
Jonathan Hide

Camb. Aprill 5 1692
Attested upon Oath before the Court
by JOHN FULLER *Senect.*
JONATHAN HIDE.
SAML PHIPPS
Clk."

John Fuller married Elizabeth ————.
He died Feb. 7, 1698, aged 78.   Wife died April 13, 1700.

CHILDREN, SECOND GENERATION.

I.   JOHN,   b. 1645.   2
II.   JONATHAN. b. 1648.   3
III. ELIZABETH, b. 1650: m. Job Hyde, 1667; d. 1700. 4
IV.   JOSEPH,   b. 1652.   5
V.   JOSHUA,   b. 1654.   6
VI.   JEREMIAH, b. 1658.   7
VII. BETHIA, b. 1661: m. N. Bond, of Watertown, 1685. 8
VIII. ISAAC, b. 1665; d. 1691.   9

2. JOHN FULLER, 2d.born 1645; married Abigail Boylston,
1682. Second wife, Margaret Hicks, October 14, 1714.   He
died 1720, aged 75 years.

CHILDREN, THIRD GENERATION.

I.   SARAH,   b. May   8, 1683.   10
II.   JOHN,   b. Sept. 2, 1685.   11
III. ABIGAIL,   b. March 8, 1688.   12
IV.   JAMES, . b. Feb.   4, 1690.   13
V.   HANNAH,   b. Aug. 31, 1693.   14
VI.   ISAAC,   b. Nov. 22, 1695.   15
VII. JONATHAN, b. Feb. 13, 1698.   16
VIII. JONATHAN, b. Mar. 28, 1700.   17
IX.   CALEB,   b. Feb. 21, 1702.   18

3. JONATHAN FULLER, son of John, born 1618; married Mindwell Trowbridge, no issue; by will he bequeathed his estate to Jonathan, son of his brother Joseph. He was selectman in Newton. Died August 12, 1722, aged 77. Widow died 1758, aged 96.

5. JOSEPH FULLER, third son of John, known as Captain Joseph Fuller, born 1652; married Dec. 13, 1680, Lydia, daughter of Edward Jackson, of Newton. His father-in-law* gave him 20 acres of land from the West end of the Mayhew farm of 500 acres which he bought of Gov. Simon Bradstreet, in 1646, for £140—which Bradstreet bought of Thomas Mayhew, of Watertown, in 1638, with the buildings, for six cows.

This tract commenced near what is now the division line between Newton and Brighton, and extended Westward, including what is now Newtonville, and covering the site of General Hull's place, now owned by Governor Claflin. Here Joseph Fuller built his house, and this 20 acres, together with about 200 inherited from his father, formed the farm which descended to his son Joseph, his grandson Abraham, and his great-granddaughter Sarah, who married William Hull. In 1814, William Hull built a new house on the same spot where Joseph Fuller's stood for one hundred and thirty years. The house built by General Hull was, after the death of his widow and the sale of the estate, removed to the railroad station called "Hull's crossing," to make room for the house built by Governor Claflin, who bought the property, and who is the third of that title who has owned it—Governor Bradstreet, Governor Hull, and Governor Claflin. The large elm tree still standing near the house, was, according to a family tradition, a riding switch planted by Joseph

---

* DEED OF GIFT—Edward Jackson to Joseph and Lydia Fuller, 1680:

"This present witnesseth, that I, Edward Jackson, have given to Joseph Fuller, and to my daughter Lidia his wife, Twenty accers of Land, lying and being vppon the South West corner of the farme which I bought of Mr. Broadstreete, and also I have soid some tenne accers more adioyning to the foresaid Twenty as it is layd out and Bounded by David Fiske of Cambridge bounds Surveyor, also I doe by these presents acknowledge that I have receaved the sume of six pounds in money in and his father John Fuller is to pay sixteene more as followeth, vppon the first of March in the yeare 1681, and five pound in the first of March 1682, and the last five pound on the first of March 1683, the which somes beeing so payd as above expressed, I doe by these presents assigne and make over to the above namd Joseph Fuller and to his heires forever, to have and to hold without any just mollestation of me my heires Executors and Administrators, or any of vs; in Witness hereof I have set to my hand and scale

John Mason,   EDWARD JACKSON.   SEAL.
Isaac Bacon.

Fuller the first; and there remained until about 1830, in the hall, a pair of deer's horns, the wearer of which was shot from his front door by the same Joseph. He was Captain of the Newton Horse Company, and in 1735 he gave a training field to them; it was situated on the road from his house to Newton corner, and was afterwards sold by the town. Joseph Fuller was Selectman for five years.

He died January 5, 1740, aged 88 years.

Wife Lydia died in 1726, aged 70 years.

CHILDREN, THIRD GENERATION.

I.	John,	b. 1681.			19
II.	Joseph,	b. July	4, 1685.		20
III.	Jonathan,	b. Jan.	7, 1686.		21
IV.	Lydia,	b. Feb.	15, 1692; m.——Stratton.		22
V.	Edward,	b. Mar.	7, 1694.		23
VI.	Isaac,	b. Mar.	16, 1698.		24
VII.	Elizabeth,	b. July 1, 1701; m. Josiah Bond, 1720.			25

6. JOSHUA FULLER, son of John, born 1654; married Elizabeth, daughter of John Ward, Jr., of Newton, in 1679.

CHILDREN, THIRD GENERATION.

I.	Elizabeth, b. Feb. 22, 1680; m. Isaac Shepard, 1702.		26
II.	Hannah, b. July 8, 1682; m. Stephen Cook, of Watertown.		27
III.	Experience, b. Nov. 5, 1685; m. Mason, and, second, John Child.		28
IV.	Mercy, b. March 11, 1689; m. Cady.		29
V.	Abigail, b. 1697; m. Joseph Garfield.		30
VI.	Sarah, b. 1699; m. Richard Park.		31
VII.	Ruth, b. 1701; m. Cheney.		32

In his eighty-eighth year, Joshua Fuller married Mary Dana, of Cambridge, aged 75.

He died June 27, 1752, aged 98.

7. Lieut. JEREMIAH FULLER, fifth son of John, born 1658; married:—1st. Mary ——, in 1688; she died 1689.

2d. Elizabeth ——; she died 1700.

3d. Thankful ——;   "   "   1729.

4th. —— ——;   "   "   1742.

He was Selectman sixteen years. Will, dated 1742, gives son Thomas ninety-two acres of land; son Jonathan, one hundred

and twenty-five acres: son Josiah, sixty-six acres. His books to be equally divided among his children. He died December 23, 1743, aged 85 years.

CHILDREN, THIRD GENERATION.

I.	Elizabeth,	b. April 14, 1694 ; d. young.	33
II.	Jeremiah,	b. July 3, 1697 ; d. in 1703.	34
III.	Thomas,	b. Sept. 12, 1701.	35
IV.	Joshua,	b. April 12, 1703.	36
V.	Thankful,	b. Dec. 23, 1704.	37
VI.	Jeremiah,	b. Nov. 1, 1707 ; d. in 1711.	38
VII.	Elizabeth,	b. Aug. 24, 1709 ; d. in 1711.	39
VIII.	Josiah,	b. Dec. 2, 1710.	40

11. JOHN FULLER, 3d, son of John 2d, born 1685 ; married Sarah ——, 1709.

CHILDREN, FOURTH GENERATION.

I.	Elizabeth,	b. June 27, 1712.	41
II.	James,	b. Feb. 9, 1715.	42
III.	Abigail,	b. April 9, 1717.	43
IV.	Mary,	b. June 2, 1720.	44
V.	Jerusha,	b. Oct. 16, 1722.	45
VI.	Rebecca,	b. Sept. 21, 1730.	46
VII.	Sarah,	b. July 8, 1733.	47
VIII.	Elisha,	b. Oct. 10, 1735.	48

15. ISAAC FULLER, son of John 2d. born 1695 ; married Hannah Greenwood in 1722. He died 1745, aged 50.

CHILDREN, FOURTH GENERATION.

I.	Susanna,	b. July 13, 1725 ; d. 1748.	49
II.	Joseph,	b. Aug. 15, 1727.	50
III.	Ruth,	b. Sept. 18, 1729 ; m. Peter Durell, 1751.	51
IV.	Lois,	b. Dec. 12, 1732 ; d. 1749.	52
V.	Tabitha,	b. Sept. 7, 1734.	53
VI.	Hannah,	b. Nov. 11, 1735.	54
VII.	Lydia,	b. Oct. 23, 1737 ; m. Daniel Fuller, 1756.	55
VIII.	Abigail, died 1753.		56

17. JONATHAN FULLER, son of John 2d, born 1700 ; married Elizabeth Woodward, 1725. He died in 1783, aged 83.

CHILDREN, FOURTH GENERATION.

I.	KESIAH,	b. Oct. 7, 1725; d. 1741.	57
II.	JONAS,	b. April 23, 1727.	58
III.	JOHN,	} twins, b. Feb. 10, 1729.	59
IV.	HANNAH,		60
V.	ELIZABETH,	b. Nov. 10, 1730: m. Sam'l Gooding, 1756.	61
VI.	DANIEL,	b. Aug. 13, 1732.	62
VII.	GRACE,	b. June 14. 1734.	63
VIII.	ELEANOR,	b. March 14, 1736.	64
IX.	AMOS,	b. Feb. 7, 1738.	65
X.	THADDEUS,	b. Feb. 17, 1740.	66
XI.	MARY,	b. Sept. 1744.	67

18. CALEB FULLER, son of John 2d, born 1702; married Temperance Hyde, of Newton, 1725. She died 1740. Second wife Mary Hovey, 1750. He died 1770, aged 68.

CHILDREN, FOURTH GENERATION.

I.	EPHRAIM,	b. Dec. 31, 1725.	68
II.	NEHEMIAH,	b. Sept. 16, 1727.	69
III.	WILLIAM,	b. June, 2, 1732.	70
IV.	BETHIA,	b. Nov. 13, 1734: m. John Murdock.	71
V.	ANNE,	b. Mar. 31, 1739.	72

20. JOSEPH FULLER, 2d son of Joseph, born 1683; married, May 11, 1719, Sarah, daughter of Abraham Jackson, of Newton. He was chosen Representative to General Court in 1749, but declined serving. Was a Selectman six years. Was Lieut. of the Newton Horse Company. He died April 23, 1766, aged 81. Will dated 1764. His wife died Nov. 21, 1754, aged 61 years.

CHILDREN, FOURTH GENERATION.

I.	ABRAHAM,	b. March 23, 1720.	73
II.	ELIZABETH,	b. Oct. 28, 1722 ; m. Rev. Isaac Jones, of Weston, 1749.	74

73. ABRAHAM FULLER, son of Joseph 2d, born 1720. During his father's lifetime he kept a private grammar school in Newton, and was also Town Clerk and Treasurer, for twenty-seven years, commencing in 1763. He was a Selectman four years; Representative to the General Court, eighteen years; Delegate to the Provincial Congress; a Senator, Councillor and

Judge of the Court of Common Pleas for Middlesex County. He was also chosen Major of the first Middlesex Regiment, in 1771.

After his father's death, in 1766, he removed to the house built by his grandfather, Capt. Joseph Fuller, and carried on the farm, adding to it the business of a maltster. At that period, when beer was the usual beverage, and was drunk at all meals, the trade in malt was a very important one; and it is related of Judge Fuller, that at one time, there being a scarcity of malt, it happened that he was the only holder of it in the town. So far from taking advantage of this, he continued to sell at the old prices, and would only allow each purchaser to have a limited quantity, lest the poor should be deprived of their beer. The old malt house where the business was carried on was standing as lately as 1825, and was occupied for lodging rooms by the farm laborers employed by General Hull.

These men had a story that the old Judge used to walk there, in his white wig, twenty years after his death. Judge Fuller was a very earnest patriot before the Revolution, and it is told that previous to the fight at Concord, fearing that the British might destroy the County Records at that place, he rode over from Newton the day before the fight, and carried away the most valuable of the papers in his saddlebags to his house in Newton.* In 1777, when about £3000 were raised in the town to pay the Newton soldiers, Judge Fuller subscribed £286 of the amount, there being only one larger subscription, that of Elnathan Winchester. In 1775, the older men of the town who were past active service, were enrolled into a company which was called the Alarm List. In this was Abraham Fuller. Three companies of Newton men, two hundred and eighteen in all, were engaged in the affair of the 19th of April.

Judge Fuller was a member of the convention which assembled in Boston, January, 1788, to ratify the Constitution of the United States, and took part in the debates. He asked this question of Elbridge Gerry, who was present to answer "questions of fact."

"Why, in the last requisition of Congress, the portion of taxes

* "To him were committed, as one of the Provincial Congress at Concord, the papers containing the exact returns of the Military Stores of Massachusetts in 1775. He wisely drew them from the cabinet where they had been kept, and carried them to his house in Newton on the day before the attack on Concord, April 19, 1775. The British officers when they entered the town searched for those papers, and expressed great disappointment at missing them."—HOMER's *History of Newton.*

2

required of this State was thirteen times as much as of Georgia, and yet we have but eight Representatives in the general government, and Georgia has three?' Until this question was answered, he was at a loss to know how taxation and representation went hand in hand."

It was voted that this question be asked of Mr. Gerry. A long and desultory debate ensued on the manner in which the answer should be given. It was finally voted that Mr. Gerry should reduce his answer to writing.

(Saturday, Jan. 19th.) Mr. Gerry's answer to Mr. Fuller's question was read. The purport was, that Georgia had increased in its number by immigration—and if it had not then, would soon be entitled to the proportion assigned her. Which seems rather a feeble reply, but it sufficed, for the Constitution was adopted in Massachusetts by a vote of 187 to 168—Judge Fuller voting aye.

By his will, July, 1793, he left £300 "for the purpose of laying the foundation of an Academy in Newton." The building was erected in the West Parish, and was used for an Academy for some years. Afterwards it was sold by the town to the Mess. Allen, who occupy it as a private school for boys.

Judge Fuller was a man of great integrity and justice; somewhat stern in aspect and manner, as became one who had been many years a teacher of youth, a Judge and a Senator. Of large, portly person, and a voice so powerful, that it is said he could be distinctly heard calling to his workmen from his farm to Angier's corner, a mile distant. Once, when the small-pox prevailed in his vicinity, he agreed with Dr. Marshall Spring, of Watertown, to call out to him the news from the top of Chestnut Hill on his farm. He went and shouted "All's well!" and Dr. Spring heard him at Watertown. He was very averse to owing even the smallest sum of money; and it is related, that when, on his death bed, seeming uneasy, his wife asked what troubled him, he replied, "I owe Lucy Harris ninepence for mending my shoe: send over and pay the money; I have never lived in debt, and I cannot die in debt." So the ninepence was paid, and the Judge departed in peace.

He had intended to have been buried on his farm; but it occurred to him, that notwithstanding the precautions of John Fuller, his ancestor, to keep the place in the family, it might be sold by his descendants: "I never was bought nor sold when alive, and I won't be sold after I die," said he, and so was buried in the family tomb in the cemetery at Newton Centre.

When this tomb was opened nine years afterwards, to admit the body of his wife, it was found that the body of Judge Fuller was in a remarkable state of preservation, being converted into a substance as hard as wood, but retaining the features so well that he would have been recognized by any person who had known him in life. The body remained in this condition for many years, and was visited by the scientific and the curious, until their visits became an annoyance to the family, when the tomb was closed by a marble door. Twenty-five years after burial, the body remained nearly perfect in form, though the coffin had mouldered away, so that it became necessary to replace it with a new one. Whatever the preserving influence was (and it has never been explained), it has ceased to act, for at a recent visit (1866) the coffin was opened, and nothing found in it excepting the bones.

Abraham Fuller married, in 1758, Sarah Dyer, of Weymouth, he being then thirty-eight years of age, and she thirty-one.

He died April 20, 1794, aged 74 years.

She died April 7, 1803, aged 76 years.

CHILDREN, FIFTH GENERATION.

I. Sarah, b. April 27, 1759; m. Col. William Hull, 1781. 75
II. Joseph, b. 1765; d. the same year. 76

75. SARAH FULLER, daughter of Abraham Fuller, born 1759; married Colonel William Hull in 1781.

He died Nov. 25, 1825, aged 72 years.

She died August 1, 1826, aged 67 years.

CHILDREN, SIXTH GENERATION.

I. Sarah Hull, b. Jan. 20, 1783; m. John McKesson, of New York. 77
II. Eliza Hull, b. June 22, 1784; m. Isaac McLellan, of Boston. 78
III. Abraham Fuller Hull, b. March 8, 1786. Harvard University 1805. Studied law. Was appointed Capt. in 9th Infantry 1811, and was killed at the battle of Lundy's Lane, July 25, 1814, aged 28. 79
IV. Anne Binney Hull, b. June 19, 1787; m. Capt. Hickman, United States Army. 80
V Maria Hull, b. June 7, 1788; m. Edward F. Campbell, of Georgia. 81

DYERS OF WEYMOUTH.

1. THOMAS DYER, cloth worker; freeman 1641: Representative to General Court, 1646 to 1650. Wife Agnes ———. She died 1647. He died 1676.

CHILDREN.

1. MARY,   b. 1641.
2. JOHN,   b. 1643.
3. THOMAS,   b. 1645.
4. ABIGAIL,   b. 1647.
5. SARAH,   b. 1649.
6. THOMAS, 2d, b. 1651.
7. JOSEPH,   } twins, b. 1653.
8. BENJAMIN,   }

2. JOSEPH DYER, born 1653; freeman in 1681. Wife Hannah ———, married in 1682.

CHILDREN.

1. HANNAH,   b. Oct. 10, 1682; d. young.
2. HANNAH,   b. Feb. 13, 1683.
3. JOSEPH,   b. Jan. 19, 1686.
4. BENJAMIN, b. April 13, 1688.
5. MARY,   b. April 12, 1690.
6. JOHN,   b. April 9, 1692.
7. THOMAS,   b. April 15, 1694.
8. MEHITABEL, b. June   9, 1700.
9. SARAH,   b. Aug. 29, 1702.

3. JOSEPH DYER, 2d, born 1686; married, 1726, Jane Stephens.

CHILDREN.

1. SARAH, b. March 20, 1727; m. 1753, Judge Fuller, of Newton.
2. JANE,   b. May   2, 1729.
3. JOSEPH, b. Sept. 7, 1733.
4. ASA,   b. July 26, 1739.
5. MARY,   b. Mar. 13, 1744.
6. JAMES, b. June 14, 1746.

ARMS OF FULLER. Barry of six, gules and arg. on a Canton of the 2d, a Castle, or.

CREST. An arm sable, holding a dagger.

Rev. Arthur Fuller, in a sketch of his family history, in the Genealogical Register, says: "These arms have been in an American family of Fullers for a long time. Burke describes the same shield as belonging to a Fuller in the Isle of Wight."

ARMS OF JOHN FULLER, of Waldron, Co. Essex, who died in 1615. Barry of six, arg. and gules. A Canton of the last.

CREST. A horse passant, arg.

MOTTO. " *Currit qui curat.*"

The present representative of the above is Augustus Eliot Fuller, of Rose Hill, Brightling, and Ashdown House, Co. Sussex, England, M. P. for East Sussex, born 1777, has issue.

Owen John Augustus Fuller, born July 13, 1894.—*Burke's Landed Gentry.*

INDEX.